Little Bear's
Christmas

Little Bear's Christmas

Norbert Landa

Illustrated by

Marlis Scharff-Kniemeyer

BLOOMSBURY
CHILDREN'S
BOOKS

It was autumn in Bear Valley. The wind ripped the bright leaves from the trees and swept them into great rustling heaps.

'I can do something you can't do!' shouted Bertie Bear gleefully. He scrambled up a tree and then let himself drop into the soft pile of leaves below.

Wolfie Wolf and Wilfred Wolf watched him.

'Autumn leaves are the best!' shouted Bertie.

'Huh!' snorted Wolfie. 'Winter snow is better.'

'Snow?' wondered Bertie. He had never heard of snow before.

'That's because you bears sleep through the winter,' said Wilfred.

'Nonsense,' growled Bertie. 'You're just jealous because you can't climb trees.'

The next day the three friends went out to fly their kites. Bertie's kite flew the highest.

'Flying kites may be fun,' said Wolfie grumpily, 'but Father Christmas is better. He brings lovely presents and we all sing Christmas carols.'

'Sing?' laughed Bertie. 'The way you wolves howl, I'd rather be asleep!'

The following morning Bertie, Wolfie and Wilfred went to gather mushrooms.

'Look, there! And here! And here!' called Bertie. 'See how many mushrooms I've found already. We'll have a delicious supper tonight.'

Wolfie and Wilfred looked glumly into their empty baskets.

'Mushrooms are yummy!' said Wilfred.

'Maybe. But honey cakes and chocolate hearts from Father Christmas are best,' said Wolfie.

That evening Bertie asked his mother to tell him all about winter, the snow and Father Christmas.

'Winter is very cold and bleak,' said Mrs Bear. 'The mushrooms and berries disappear, and even the rain freezes. It turns white and settles on the ground, and people call it snow. Sensible people, like us bears, go to bed and stay there until the warm spring arrives.'

'And what about Father Christmas?' asked Bertie.

'I was coming to him,' said Mrs Bear. 'People who don't sleep through the winter aren't as lucky as we are. They have to trudge about in the cold snow. Father Christmas gives them something to look forward to in the dark days of winter.'

'What does he look like?'

'Well, I've never seen him, but people say he wears a red coat and has a white beard.'

Mrs Bear gave Bertie a big hug and sang him a lullaby.

'I suppose we bears do have to sleep through Christmas,' thought Bertie afterwards, 'but I so want to see Father Christmas. I think I know how to, as well. If I try to sleep as much as I can now, I'll be wide awake for Christmas!'

The next morning Bear Valley was shrouded in fog. Then it started to rain. Wolfie and Wilfred sailed their boats in the puddles, but Bertie stayed in bed.

'What's the matter?' asked Mrs Bear. 'Aren't you feeling well?'

'No, I'm fine,' said Bertie. 'I just want to sleep a little longer.'

'Sleep? At this time of day?' Mrs Bear was worried and called Dr Wolf.

Dr Wolf checked Bertie's tongue and took his temperature.

'This little one's fine,' he said. 'Perhaps the weather is making him tired. I can feel snow coming. I'm sure he'll be bright as a button by Christmas.'

Christmas? Bertie listened hard.

'Shhh, Doctor,' whispered Mrs Bear. 'Remember, we bears sleep through the winter.'

'Of course you do,' said the doctor. 'Well, sleep soundly.'

Dr Wolf hurried home. It was growing very cold, and dark clouds hung over Bear Valley. Snow was on its way.

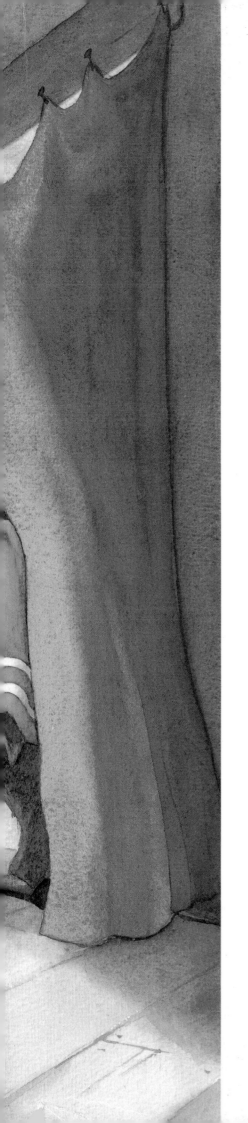

A few days later Mrs Bear prepared the cottage for their winter sleep. She tied thick ropes around a sack of grain and hung it from the ceiling to keep it safe from the greedy mice. Then Mrs Bear locked the door, closed the shutters, and yawned.

'Time for bed,' she said, giving Bertie a good night kiss. 'Sleep well, little cub, until springtime.' Mrs Bear went into her bedroom, but came out again almost immediately. 'Have you seen my alarm clock?' she asked. Bertie lay as still as he could.

'Goodness, he's fast asleep already!' said Mrs Bear to herself. 'Never mind. I don't need an alarm clock. The spring sunshine will wake us up.' She tiptoed out of the room.

Bertie giggled quietly. 'I've hidden the alarm clock under my bed! It'll wake me up at Christmas – and then . . .' Bertie fell asleep.

In the valley the snow began to fall in thick, white flakes. The air was still. It was very peaceful. Inside the cottage the little bear slept for a very long time.

Suddenly the alarm clock shrilled. Bertie nearly fell out of bed with surprise. What a noise! He turned it off hurriedly. Had Mrs Bear heard it too? No, all Bertie could hear was Mrs Bear's gentle snoring. He threw open the shutters and looked out.

What a miracle! Someone had covered the whole of the valley
with a white, fluffy blanket, as thick and soft as a featherbed. So
this was snow! And, thought Bertie, where there's snow, Father
Christmas can't be far away.

Bertie tied on his scarf, opened the door and stepped out into the
shining white snow. He listened. He couldn't hear a sound.

'I'm going to find Father Christmas!' whispered Bertie and
plodded up the hill. Every step left a small, deep paw-print.
The snow felt fluffy, but it wasn't as warm as a featherbed.
In fact, it was very cold. Amazing!

At last the little bear reached the top of the hill. From here he could see across the whole valley. Bertie looked in all directions. Where was Father Christmas?

Then he felt something cold and wet on his nose. A snowflake! And another one! Snowflakes came dancing down from the sky and Bertie danced with them until he was dizzy.

By the time Bertie stopped for breath there were so many whirling snowflakes that he could hardly see past his nose.

'Father Christmas, where are you?' he shouted. 'Can you hear me?'

But Father Christmas didn't answer.

Everything was silent.

The snow continued to flutter down from the sky. Bertie waited. His feet were getting cold. Then he began to feel hungry. And soon he started to feel frightened. Darkness was falling.

'How can I find Father Christmas in the dark?' sighed Bertie. 'I'd better go home while I can still find my way.'

The little bear slid down the hill, following the paw-prints he had left before. But the snow fell thickly and soon his paw-prints were covered over. Now Bertie didn't know where he was, or how to find his way home.

'Help!' shouted Bertie. 'I want to go home!'

Bertie strained his ears to catch any sound. He could hear nothing except a distant howling. Could that be Wolfie and Wilfred singing? No, it was only the wind. But then Bertie heard a faint tinkling and a sleigh appeared through the snowflakes.

'Hey! Stop!' shouted the little bear. 'Please, wait for me!'

The driver pulled on his reins and turned round. He was wrapped from head to toe in a thick blanket and Bertie could see only a friendly face with twinkling blue eyes. The little bear stepped nearer and stared, astonished. The sleigh had no wheels! It sped across the snow on huge skis, pulled by reindeer with magnificent antlers.

'Hallo, Bertie!' cried the driver. 'Where have you come from? Shouldn't little bears be asleep now?'

'Well, yes, they should really,' murmured Bertie, embarrassed, 'but I wanted to find Father Christmas, and now I can't find my way home!'

'I thought so,' laughed the driver. 'Come with me - and hold tight!'

Bertie climbed aboard, amazed. 'Giddy up!' shouted the
driver, and the reindeer gave a mighty leap. In no time the
sleigh was flying through the air. Bertie was scared. The
valley floor seemed so far below them. 'Hey! Where are
we going?' he called out nervously.

'We're taking you home, of course!'

In no time the sleigh swept back to earth and landed right in
front of the cottage. The driver leapt down from his seat and
threw off the blanket. Now Bertie could see that he was
wearing a red coat!

'Y-y-you're Father Christmas...' stammered the little bear.

' Of course I am,' whispered Father Christmas. 'But quiet now or
you'll wake up your mother.' Father Christmas pulled the cloth off the
sleigh and Bertie saw a huge heap of packets and parcels and presents.

'Now, what would you like for Christmas?' asked Father Christmas.

Bertie thought hard. 'I'll have - honey cakes and chocolate hearts.
And for Mummy ... chocolate hearts and honey cakes!'

'Good,' said Father Christmas. He rummaged about in the sleigh and
at last pulled out two squashy parcels. Together they carried the
presents to the bears' cottage.

'I must go now,' whispered
Father Christmas.

'Wolfie and Wilfred are waiting
for me. And I'll tell you what, next Christmas
I'll bring you presents – but only if you're asleep,
all right?'

'All right,' agreed Bertie.

He watched as Father Christmas scrambled back up into the driver's seat. Then the sleigh shot off so fast that it sent sparks flying. Soon he could only see it as a tiny speck in the dark sky. Or was that a star? Bertie was much too tired to think about it now. He tiptoed into his room, hid the parcels in his toy chest and crawled into bed.

Then he slept.

When Bertie woke up it was daylight. He could smell flowers. Birds were twittering. Mrs Bear had thrown open the windows.

'Good morning, little one!' cried Mrs Bear, kissing Bertie on the nose. 'Time to get up! It's springtime!'

Springtime? Bertie rubbed his eyes and yawned. Then he remembered. 'Father Christmas was here!'

'The mice were here, you mean,' called Mrs Bear from the kitchen. 'Look what they've done to our sack of grain. They've chewed through the ropes and have eaten every scrap! What will we have for breakfast?'

'Honey cakes and chocolate hearts!' shouted Bertie, running to his toy box. 'And chocolate hearts and honey cakes!' Then he told Mrs Bear the whole story.

'And the best thing is - Father Christmas will come again next year!' finished the little bear.

'Yes,' agreed Mrs Bear, 'but only if you're asleep!'

A little later Wolfie and Wilfred peeped through the windows.
They sniffed the air curiously.

'That's funny!' they said. 'Your house smells all Christmassy!'

Mrs Bear and Bertie winked at one another. 'We bears
always celebrate Christmas a little late,' they said.
'Didn't you know?'

First published in Great Britain 1997 by Bloomsbury Publishing Plc
38 Soho Square London W1V 5DF
All rights reserved; no part of this publication may be reproduced or transmitted by any means, electronic, mechanical, pho-
tocopying or otherwise, without the prior permission of the publisher
A CIP catalogue record for this book is available from the British Library
First published 1997 by Ravensburger Buchverlag as Wo bist du, Weihnachtsmann?
Copyright © Ravensburger Buchverlag
Illustrations by Marlis Scharff-Kniemeyer
Text byNorbert Landa
English translation by Anna Trenter
ISBN 0747 5 3767 4
10 9 8 7 6 5 4 3 2 1
Printed in Germany